# "Dear Millie"

## A Comedy in One Act for Six Women

## by Fred Carmichael

Baker's Plays
7611 Sunset Blvd.
Los Angeles, CA 90042
bakersplays.com

# STORY OF THE PLAY

"*Dear Millie*" is the title of a Lonely Hearts column which Millie Tyson writes She has a summer home in New England close to her three best friends They have decided that Millie is getting a little too conceited with her advice-giving and devise a plot where they will confide in her that each of their husbands is secretly seeing their best friends Millie is no one's fool and artfully turns the tables on them before her secretary brings about another surprise—twist ending The sixth character is a country maid who has problems of her own The dialogue is bright and witty and the plot full of surprises

# CHARACTERS

Betty

Eloise Matthews

Lucille Jamison

Josephine Kramer

Millie Tyson

Julia Corley

Scene   Living room of the Tyson home.

Time   The present  Summer

# "DEAR MILLIE"

*(The curtain opens to show us a living room in a country home It is a homey and comfortable room in the house of Millie Tyson U C is an archway which leads to the outside door off L and to the kitchen and the rest of the house off R A small table stands to the R of the archway with a bottle of sherry and some glasses on it D R is a pair of French windows which lead to the outside and the gardens R stage is a woman's desk with chair matching it on the R side of it The desk is almost perpendiculor to the audience but is on a slight C angle To the L of the desk is a rather comfortable straight chair There are the usual necessities of working life on the desk and an extremely large pile of mail On stage L is a comfortable sofa with a small table to the left of it An easy chair is below the table and to the left of it Attractive and feminine paintings cover the walls* NOTE *The play can easily be presented in drapes as it is not necessary for any of the doors to be practical )*

BETTY (*Off stage* L ) You can wait in the parlor, Mrs Matthews (*She enters followed by* ELOISE MATTHEWS. BETTY *is a young country domestic She speaks with a country accent and is most of the time cheery with what life has to offer She wears a cotton dress with an apron over it* ELOISE *is in her late forties The time is summer and she is smartly dressed as if she were about to go to the Club or a fashion show* ) I don't rightly know when Mrs Tyson will be back She just said Tuesday.

ELOISE (*Removes her gloves and crosses above desk, putting the gloves in her purse*) The way *she* drives she can make it from New York in four hours. Anyone else would take seven

BETTY Not with that Jackal she's got

ELOISE (*Pauses in her movement*) Betty, it's a Jaguar.

BETTY I know'd it was some kind of animal

ELOISE It's remarkable, Betty, how like your sister you are.

BETTY (*Moves* D C) Hyacinth and me is sometimes taken for twins 'cept she's eleven months older than me She says we got a better kitchen than you

ELOISE (*Crosses above desk to French windows and indicates the gardens*) And a better garden and a better view and your mistress makes more money than my husband.

BETTY But Mrs Tyson works real hard for it It takes her and Miss Kramer a whole morning every day just to answer the mail (*Indicates piles of mail on desk*) To say nothing of all the time they spend writing that column. I sure wouldn't be bright enough to do that

ELOISE No, Betty, but the average person would

BETTY Yes, ma'am (*Thinks a minute to decide whether she has been insulted or not*)

ELOISE When you write a Lonely Hearts column, all you have to do is answer questions (*Sits* L *of desk*) If there aren't any good questions, you just make them up

BETTY Mrs Tyson, don't never do that It'd be dishonest

ELOISE (*Takes cigarette from her purse*) I must say I respect her for working I don't know what I'd do if my husband died and left me without any insurance I'd never be able to get a job good enough to keep up the place in the city and come to New Hampshire every summer (*Lights cigarette*)

BETTY I sure hope I marry someone rich My Dellwood ain't, he's just a hand on Mr Simon's farm He got a raise, though Now he's driving the manure spreader

ELOISE That sounds delightful

BETTY It's all right, of course. but after he's had a hard day in the fields, I gotta be sure and walk on the windward side of him

ELOISE And pray for a steady breeze

BETTY (*Starts for door*) Would you like me to mix you one of them cocktail things, Mrs Matthews?

ELOISE It's too early. Besides, your martinis are one to one I'll settle for a sherry Did any of the other girls phone today?

BETTY (*Pours sherry at table* U R) You mean Mrs Corley or Mrs Jamison? Not yet

ELOISE I suppose I shouldn't call us girls, should I?

BETTY Well, it does sound funny like (*Brings sherry to* ELOISE)

ELOISE I suppose I still think we're together in dancing school It doesn't seem long ago we were all in each other's weddings, paced the waiting rooms in hospitals when one of us was having a baby We've built each other up and pulled each other down when one of us needed it We all live within nine blocks in New York and we all have summer homes within ten miles up here And to each other, we're still girls (*Has crossed to sofa during above*)

BETTY You knew Mrs Tyson even before she wrote the column?

ELOISE I knew Millie when she failed penmanship in the fifth grade (*Sits sofa*)

BETTY She don't have to worry now Miss Kramer types the column

ELOISE When her husband was alive, Millie dabbled with writing children's books, those things like "Nancy-Prancy Meets Chicky-Chick" and "Nancy-Prancy Meets Ducky-Duck" and "Nancy-Prancy Meets Godzilla" (BETTY *laughs*) Then this Dear Millie column came along, after her husband died, and she gave it a try Whoever would have thought it would come to this, syndicated throughout the country, two best-seller books out of it? Next thing, they'll have "I Love Millie" T-shirts for teenagers

BETTY I'd buy one and have her autograph it It's fun working for an important person

ELOISE (*Puts her glass on table by sofa*) Even one who knows it?

BETTY Oh, Mrs Tyson ain't conceited

ELOISE (*Sarcastic*) Uh-huh (*Rises and crosses to French windows*) You don't have to stay and entertain me, Betty I'll just wait a few more minutes

BETTY OK If you want Miss Kramer, she's down in the garden by the cosmos I told her Dellwood could come over and help her but she says she's spread her own manure for years

ELOISE She's reviewing the column

BETTY (*Crosses to* U C) Well, I'll get back to my

kitchen. If my apple pie has dropped, I'll just flip it over and call it an upside-down cake. (*Exits to kitchen* )

> (ELOISE *puts her cigarette out in ash tray on desk and starts going through the mail on the desk  Doorbell rings* )

ELOISE  I'll get it, Betty
BETTY  (*Off stage*) That's good.
ELOISE  (*Goes out and to the* L ) Lucille, it's—
LUCILLE  (*Off stage*) Oh, Eloise. (LUCILLE CORLEY *enters  She is the same age as* ELOISE *and obviously rather well off  At the moment, she is in a state  She has a handkerchief to her eyes  She leans* U. C *and speaks very dramatically.*) My life is over  The future is doomed  I face old age, sad and embittered (*Buries her face in the handkerchief* )
ELOISE  (*Has entered and regards* LUCILLE) Millie isn't here yet
LUCILLE  (*Drops the handkerchief and the dramatics*) Oh
ELOISE  (*Crosses below* LUCILLE *to above the table for her sherry*) You can save the histrionics
LUCILLE  I was doing well, though, wasn't I? I really felt the part like I was Joan Crawford in one of those movies where she's lost Spencer Tracy
ELOISE  Lucille, I think the hand to the forehead was more Theda Bara, wasn't it?
LUCILLE  Don't criticize me  Remember when I was in high school, I played Portia in The Merchant of Wherever-it-was  Where's Millie?
ELOISE  (*Sits in the chair* D L ) She hasn't gotten home yet. Have some sherry
LUCILLE  I need it! (*Pours herself some* ) Maybe this isn't such a good idea after all.
ELOISE  Nonsense, Lucille, it's the best practical joke we've ever thought of. Besides, Millie's getting a little too conceited about this Lonely Hearts business  She needs to be taken down a peg
LUCILLE  (*Crosses* C  *Starts giggling*) It will really be wonderful if it works, though. I can't wait to see her face

ELOISE  But you'd better underplay a little

LUCILLE  I have never been accused of that

ELOISE  No, dear, you haven't

LUCILLE  (*Sits on the sofa*) I wish we had the lines written down for us  I'm much better at learned pieces than improvising

ELOISE  We can't write down the lines because we don't know what Millie will say  Just keep the basic plot in mind and you'll be fine

LUCILLE  I'd be so embarrassed coming to Millie for help if it were all true

ELOISE  It's so far-fetched, Millie is bound to believe it.

LUCILLE  (*Laughs*) Can't you just see me meeting your husband for a clandestine rendezvous? Fred and me together being romantic—it's ludicrous.

ELOISE  And what's wrong with Fred?

LUCILLE  Nothing, darling  He's an angel

ELOISE  And what about me going out with Julia's husband? Franklin's so pudgy  Another year and he'll be as bald as a billiard ball

LUCILLE  And Julia with my husband  Why, Ford would never give her a second look

ELOISE  Oh, I don't know  The girls at the beauty parlor say he's the kind with a wandering eye

LUCILLE  (*Rises and crosses* C ) Ford? Don't be ridiculous  (*Pauses as she begins to doubt* ) What have you heard—exactly?

ELOISE  Nothing, darling  Not a thing, but where there's smoke    .

LUCILLE  I want to know who's doing the smoking

ELOISE  I haven't the faintest idea  Thank heavens I'm safe with Fred  Him you can trust

LUCILLE  Why not? He's gotten that middle-age spread (*Replaces her sherry glass on the table* U R ) He doesn't exercise at the Club like Ford does  Ford says while he and Franklin are doing push-ups, the only thing Fred is raising is another martini

ELOISE  He's just jealous

LUCILLE  (*Crosses above desk  Gives a fake laugh*) Ha! Ha! Ha!

ELOISE  (*Rises and crosses* C ) Now, stop it, Lucille, this isn't the time to gossip  Let's both admit no one knows what a husband does when he isn't around but they're good providers.

LUCILLE  (*Crosses to French windows*) I agree

ELOISE  (*Puts her glass on table* U R ) The thing is we must make Millie fall for our stories  She's got to believe each of our husbands is having secret meetings with one of us  She'll be confused, she'll try to have a little talk with each of us  It'll be delicious

LUCILLE  I think the whole plan is marvelous but why do we have to pretend we're going to art classes?

ELOISE  (*Crosses below sofa*) Don't be stupid  Can any of the three of us draw a straight line?

LUCILLE  Not even with a ruler !

ELOISE  So we tell Millie that each of us is taking art lessons but that's really an excuse to meet the other one's husband at Lookout Rock

LUCILLE  (*Moves below desk*) Did you ever think of writing for "True Romances"?

ELOISE  Leave the writing to Millie

LUCILLE  (*Crosses U C to archway*) If she ever gets here  (*Turns*) What about Julia? Where is she?

ELOISE  (*Crosses below desk to* R *of it*) Maybe we ought to phone her  We shouldn't all be here together  If we are, we can't tell our stories to Millie privately  (*Holds receiver of phone towards* LUCILLE ) You phone Julia and tell her to wait another ten minutes or so.

LUCILLE  (*Crosses to* L *of desk*) You phone her  You're the chief of this gang

ELOISE  (*Dials four numbers*) All right  I always have to end up doing everything  When we were campfire girls, I was the only one who could make a fire in the rain without matches

LUCILLE  There was that one time I did and then the Chief caught me using Mother's cigarette lighter

(JOSEPHINE KRAMER *enters  She is* MILLIE'S *secretary and friend, a little younger than the others, bright and efficient  She has been gardening and is in a cotton dress, her hair a little untidy and obviously she is quite* **warm** )

Jo  Oh, good morning  Betty didn't tell me you were here

ELOISE  (*Into phone*) Hello       Oh, sorry, wrong number  (*Hangs up quickly*)

LUCILLE  (*Trying to help* ELOISE)  My, the phone service certainly is bad lately, isn't it?

Jo  I never seem to have any trouble  Millie isn't back yet

ELOISE  We know

Jo  (*Crosses below desk to* U C)  I've just been doing some weeding, but it got so hot out there, I'm completely dehydrated  I've got a thing for this New Hampshire spring water, anyway

ELOISE  Water's fattening

LUCILLE  I wish they'd make dietetic water.

Jo  You girls don't have to worry  You always look lovely

ELOISE  } We agree  (*They all laugh*)
LUCILLE  }

ELOISE  Heavens, Jo, don't stop on our account  Far be it from us to take up your time, or rather Millie's time she's paying you for  We'd just about decided to leave, anyway

Jo  If you don't mind  I do want to finish that one border of nasturtiums before Millie gets here

ELOISE  (*Goes to her and politely starts edging her towards the door*)  Run along, then  Have your water  We'll be perfectly all right

Jo  You're sure?

LUCILLE  (*Trying to be nonchalant, she crosses* R *of desk*)  Positive

(ELOISE *gives* Jo *the final slight push and she exits towards the kitchen*)

ELOISE  That was close  Poor Julia  (*Dials again from* L *of desk*)  I don't know what she must have thought.

LUCILLE  Maybe she's mad  I'd be angry if you hung up on me

ELOISE  (*Into phone*)  Julia, it's Eloise again, darling.  I know I didn't get the wrong number, but we're at

Millie's and Jo just came in          Look, Millie isn't here
yet. Lucille's here with me and we thought we'd better go
and come back when Millie's here. You know, one at a
time    . . What?

LUCILLE  What is it?

ELOISE  She says

LUCILLE  (*Can't stand it another minute, grabs the
phone*) What are you saying, Julia?          Perfect (*To
ELOISE*) She says we can park down by the brook and
when we see Millie's car come in we can follow

ELOISE  (*Grabs phone back*) Good work, Julia  .  .
What?

LUCILLE  (*Takes phone back again*) What is it? . . .
(*To* ELOISE) She forgot where we were supposed to have
the rendezvous—

ELOISE  (*Takes phone back again*) Lookout Rock  (*To
LUCILLE*) She thought it was the Municipal Reservoir
Picnic Grounds.

LUCILLE  Doesn't sound very romantic

ELOISE  (*Into phone*) Yes, Julia, you pretend you're
carrying on with Ford, Lucille is with Fred, and I'm with
your poor Franklin          What? (LUCILLE *grabs for
phone, but* ELOISE *hangs on*) No, you don't  I can answer
her questions  You're a hog  (*Into phone*) Not you, darling  I said Lucille is a hog  (*To* LUCILLE) She agrees

LUCILLE  I don't know how this whole thing started

ELOISE  (*Into phone*) No, Julia, we can't  (*To* LU-
CILLE) She wants another rehearsal.

LUCILLE  So do I.

ELOISE  (*Into phone*) We ran through the whole thing
at the pool yesterday  All we have to do is make Millie
believe we're carrying on with each other's husbands  Just
be convincing, Julia, the way you are when you make your
report for the Dried Grass Section of the Garden Club

LUCILLE  Tell her not to overplay.

ELOISE  (*Into phone*) Lucille says not to overplay  . . .
What? (*Laughs.*)

LUCILLE  What did she say?

ELOISE  It's best you never know  (*Surprised and alert,
she listens into the phone again*) She is? (*To* LUCILLE)

Millie's Jaguar just whizzed by Julia's house . . (*Into phone*) Good luck, darling (*Hangs up*)

LUCILLE (*Moves* D R ) I'm so nervous This is the first time I've acted since "The Merchant" (*She moves to below sofa*) "The quality of mercy is not stained."

ELOISE Strained, darling.

JO (*Re-enters from kitchen*) Now I can go on weeding for another half hour You know, we ought to bottle that water We could sell it in the city Call it Pep-O

ELOISE (*Grabs her purse and crosses* U C ) We're off now.

LUCILLE (*Crosses to* Jo's *left*) We'll stop by later

ELOISE Say, Jo, don't tell Millie we were here She'll be angry we didn't stay and wait

LUCILLE A good point

ELOISE I thought so Come on.

LUCILLE See you later, Jo

JO (*Moves above desk*) If I survive my bout with nature I think I've won if this isn't the summer of the seven year locust

ELOISE Good luck (*She exits hurriedly with* LUCILLE *leaving a rather confused* Jo *behind*)

JO (*Slowly crosses towards French windows, puzzled*) Hmm

BETTY (*Comes in quite agitated She is on the verge of tears*) Miss Kramer

JO Yes, Betty

BETTY I'm in trouble.

JO Did your dessert drop?

BETTY (*Comes into the room further*) Worse than that. I'm dishonest and I don't know how to tell Mrs. Tyson.

JO Betty, what have you done?

BETTY You remember last week when you went to visit your aunt over to Providence?

JO Yes (*Sits in the desk chair* )

BETTY (*Crosses above desk*) You know how Mrs Tyson says I can use the other car, the little one, whenever I have to?

JO The Hillman.

BETTY Well, me and Dellwood, we went to that charity thing over to Woods Mills—the Swimming Pool Carnival.

Well, it was so crowded we couldn't find nowheres to park except by this sign that said we shouldn't but we did

Jo  Can't Dellwood read?

Betty  (*Moves away* L) It's not that, Miss Kramer  I told him they'd never check the cars at a benefit affair like that, but they did and now I'll be in the paper  You know how they list all the people who got tickets on page 7 every Thursday  Mrs  Tyson will see it and she won't never let me use the car again  (*Cries and sinks on the sofa*) I'll be a criminal

Jo  (*Rises*) Haven't you ever gotten a ticket before?

Betty  Gracious, no  My record is as clean as Cinderella's  Now I'll be a marked woman

Jo  (*Moves to* Betty) I wouldn't worry too much about it  You confess to Mrs  Tyson when she gets here and I'll bet she forgives you

Betty  (*Rises, a smile creeping across her face*) You think so?

Jo  It's her job to help people in trouble

Betty  That's right  She'll know what to do

Millie  (*Her voice is heard off stage* L) Anyone home?

Jo  There she is now  (*Crosses to French windows*) You tell her your problem and I'll pull a few more weeds and try to figure out the answer to mine

Betty  You're in trouble, too?

Jo  I just have to decide whether to do something or not

Betty  Why don't you tell Mrs  Tyson?

Jo  That's what I'm trying to decide

Millie  (*Off stage*) Betty! Jo!

Jo  I'll give you fifteen minutes

Betty  Thanks, Miss Kramer  (Jo *goes out French windows*  Betty *calls*) I'm in here, Mrs  Tyson  (*Dabs her eyes with her handkerchief*)

Millie  (*Enters* U  C *from off* L  *She is the same age as the other girls, possibly a little less sophisticated looking at first impression  She is very intelligent and has a twinkling personality  She takes off her hat and gloves during the ensuing*) I don't know why anyone likes the city  Everyone lives on top of each other like a triple-decker sandwich  How are you, Betty? (Betty *sniffs*) Your hay fever acting up again? Maybe you're allergic to Dellwood Where's Jo? (*Her purse goes on the desk*)

BETTY She's weeding

MILLIE Back to nature Good for her (*Crosses to French windows*)

BETTY (*Steps in*) Mrs Tyson

MILLIE Yes (*Turns*) Betty, something *is* wrong

BETTY Oh, yes, ma'am Terrible wrong

MILLIE (*Sits down at her desk*) Then just tell me about it, dear I'll pretend you're writing me a letter and I'll answer you

BETTY (*Moves into desk*) Well, Mrs Tyson, this is very difficult for me to say

MILLIE Just sit down and say it simply, Betty I'll be receptive

BETTY (*Sits on chair L of desk*) Mrs Tyson, I'm in the worst trouble

MILLIE You're in trouble? (*Shocked*) Oh, Betty, you mean—?

BETTY Yes, ma'am I made a mistake and I'm going to have to pay for it (*Starts to cry again*)

MILLIE Now, don't cry I get hundreds of letters from girls in trouble You're not alone in this, Betty.

BETTY I know Dellwood was there, too

MILLIE So, it was Dellwood!

BETTY But it's not his fault It was my idea.

MILLIE How noble! But you mustn't take all the blame

BETTY There was a sign right there saying we shouldn't

MILLIE (*Rises*) A sign!

BETTY But I said no one would mind especially at a charity affair

MILLIE (*Crosses above* BETTY) Where did this happen?

BETTY At the Swimming Pool Carnival Oh, Mrs Tyson, I feel just awful about it.

MILLIE Did you tell Dellwood?

BETTY He was there when I got the ticket

MILLIE (*Moves to L of* BETTY) Ticket?

BETTY The police said it was unlawful in front of a fireplug

MILLIE Betty, what are you talking about?

BETTY  The ticket the police gave us for parking at the Carnival

MILLIE  And *that's* your problem?

BETTY  I'm a criminal  (*She rises*)

MILLIE  (*Crosses L and laughs*) Betty.

BETTY  I don't think it's funny

MILLIE. It's such a relief, I'd be happy if you robbed a bank

BETTY  What do you mean?

MILLIE  Never mind, Betty. Just pay the ticket and think no more about it  You won't even get on the police blotter

BETTY  Really?

MILLIE  Positively

BETTY  And you're not mad?

MILLIE  Of course not  (*Doorbell rings*) Now, dry your eyes and answer the door

BETTY  Yes, ma'am  (*Stops in U C archway*) Oh, Mrs Tyson, thank you  Just think, I got your advice and I didn't even have to write for it and pay five cents for a stamp  (*She exits off to L  MILLIE puts her purse and gloves in a desk drawer  LUCILLE appears U C same as before with handerchief to face  BETTY passes through archway with a peculiar look at LUCILLE*)

LUCILLE  Oh, Millie  Thank heavens you're here  My life is over. The future is doomed  I face old age sad and embittered

MILLIE  (*Crosses to LUCILLE*) Lucille, what's happened?

LUCILLE  I don't know where else to turn  I even thought of my sleeping pills, but that's the coward's way  (*She cries*)

MILLIE  Lucille! (*Helps her to sit on sofa*) Come, sit down

LUCILLE  That this should happen to me  And my best friend— Oh, I should have known. It's always the best friend  And right under my nose.

MILLIE. (*Sits beside her*) What are you talking about?

LUCILLE  Don't tell me you didn't know? I thought everyone did. Isn't the wife the last to find out? They're all laughing at me  I'll never be able to show my face at the Club again or at least not without dark glasses.

MILLIE  Now stop it, Lucille, and tell me what's wrong.

LUCILLE  I've lost Ford.

MILLIE  Lucille, he's not dead?

LUCILLE  Worse than that! He's turned into a second Casanova.

MILLIE  Your husband?

LUCILLE  Is it so impossible? He's attractive, isn't he?

MILLIE  Yes, of course

LUCILLE  He's been carrying on behind my back all Summer long

MILLIE  I don't believe it.

LUCILLE  I know it for a fact. And with— Oh, Millie, this is the cruelest blow of all

MILLIE  With whom?

LUCILLE  Julia!

MILLIE  (*Rises*) Julia Corley?

LUCILLE  The very one. That—Cleopatra!

MILLIE  (*Moves* L) Now, Lucille, are you sure this isn't just your suspicious nature?

LUCILLE  I know it for a fact. I was at the beauty parlor and I was having a mud pack  Well, there I was, sitting with this stuff all over my face and, of course, no one could recognize me, and right in the next booth I heard two women talking

MILLIE  (*Crosses above sofa*) You eavesdropped?

LUCILLE  I couldn't help it  My ears are like radar. They were talking about this married man carrying on with Julia  Of course I didn't believe it  I mean, Julia's my very best friend, except you, of course, dear  I didn't want to listen  I tried to find some cotton to stuff in my ears but I couldn't move or my mud would have cracked. So I just sat there helpless and listened  I couldn't help myself.

MILLIE  You poor soul

LUCILLE  And suddenly they said it was my Ford Julia was meeting secretly  Well, when I heard *that* my mud cracked right down the center of my nose and I just fled into the street and drove right home. I was hysterical.

MILLIE  (*Gives* LUCILLE *an unseen, suspicious look and moves* L) Of course.

LUCILLE  I'd hardly gotten inside the house when Ford came in. I never cleaned up so fast in my life  I threw the beauty parlor cape under the sofa, stuffed the left-over mud into my potted philodendron and greeted Ford as if nothing had happened

MILLIE  (*Sits in chair* L *of sofa*) And you've never mentioned it to him? That was wise

LUCILLE  Wait. I'm not through  He said he wasn't going to play golf, he'd changed his mind and was going fishing instead  Now, Millie, you know the only time he goes fishing is early in the morning  He took up his rod and reel and went off in the car  (*Rises*) But he didn't take a hook with him  Not even a bent pin!

MILLIE  That's just circumstantial evidence

LUCILLE  (*Crosses* C) Wait till I tell you about the next day  (*She has the stage and acts to her heart's content*) I was prepared  A woman scorned, you know  I borrowed Susan's red wig and put on my harlequin sun-glasses and when Ford went out, ostensibly to bowl—you know, he can't even lift a bowling ball with his slipped disc—I followed him  (*Crosses above sofa*) Do you know where he went? Lookout Rock! And Julia was there waiting for him  They went down the Nature Walk with a picnic basket and a bottle of Chianti  (*Moves* C) It was exactly the same as we used to do when he was courting me  (*Front*) Except it was a frankfurter and a coke at Far Rockaway

MILLIE  I can hardly believe it  I wonder if Julia's husband knows.

LUCILLE  Franklin's too dumb to suspect a thing  Can you imagine Franklin thinking Julia would cheat on him? And she has her excuses all set up beautifully

MILLIE  What excuses?

LUCILLE  (*Moves below sofa*) I phoned Franklin right away and asked whether Julia was in  He said she wasn't, that she'd gone for her art lesson

MILLIE  Julia taking art lessons?

LUCILLE  (*Crosses* C) How could Franklin fall for that? Julia doesn't know a Picasso from a DiMaggio.

MILLIE  (*Rises*) Maybe Ford's at the dangerous age  I write a lot about that in my column

LUCILLE  (*Collapses on sofa*) You help everyone, Milhe, complete strangers  Can you help a friend?  Tell me what to do

MILLIE  You mustn't be impetuous, Lucille  You must think, show Ford mercy

LUCILLE  That quality is too strained for me

MILLIE  (*Crosses c and speaks tentatively*) I've found the advice that works best is to make yourself more attractive for your husband  He's probably wandering because you've let yourself go to seed

LUCILLE  I—what?

MILLIE  We might as well face it, Lucille  You're not as chic as you used to be  You have a little roll of fat here and there, your hair isn't a good color this season  It's the little trees that make a forest

LUCILLE  (*Rises indignantly*) I didn't come here for you to tell me what was wrong with me

MILLIE  We must solve a problem at its root, no matter how much it hurts  (*Doorbell rings*)  This is no time for company  (*Starts u c*)  I'll tell Betty to say I'm out

(BETTY *crosses from* u r *to* u l *for the door*)

LUCILLE  (*Crosses in c*)  No, it's all right  I'll have to think about what you've said before I know what to do

JULIA  (*Off stage l*)  Betty, is Mrs. Tyson in?  She has to be. Tell me she is

LUCILLE  Julia!

BETTY  (*Off stage*)  She's in the living room

LUCILLE  I can't see Julia now  I simply can't

MILLIE  Just pretend you know nothing

LUCILLE  No  I have to compose myself  (*Crosses to French windows.*)  I'll—I'll wait in the garden  Let me know when she's gone. (*She exits*)

MILLIE  But, Lucille—  (MILLIE *looks puzzled and turns to* u c *as* JULIA *enters  She is the same age as the others and is quite striking  She is pretending a very intense feeling at the moment*  BETTY *crosses* u c *and off* r)

JULIA  Thank heavens you're back  (*Grabs* MILLIE's *hand in both of hers*)

MILLIE  Hello, Julia, how nice of you to come by  I brought you back that carrot juice and prune cake you wanted from Ye Olde Health Bar

JULIA. (*Moves away* L ) I couldn't care less  I may never eat again  Or, if I do, it will be piles of mashed potatoes drowned in thick gravy.

MILLIE  You're off your diet?

JULIA  (*Turns to* MILLIE) Look at me  Just look at me, Millie

MILLIE  I'm looking

JULIA  What do you see?

MILLIE  An attractive, happy matron.

JULIA  How little you know what's underneath the surface.

MILLIE  You're wearing a new girdle?

JULIA  Don't be crass, Millie  (*Starts pacing* D L ) Behind this calm mask I am a seething volcano of fury  You better stand back, I'm going to explode any minute.

MILLIE  What *is* the matter?

JULIA  The matter?  What's the worst thing that could happen?

MILLIE  You lost the ladies' golf trophy to Cora Hayden?

JULIA  (*Moves in a few steps*) I shall never play golf again. I'm going into a convent, an old ladies' home, somewhere. I'll devote the rest of my life to worthy charities

MILLIE  (*Moves* D C ) What's brought on this unselfish attitude?

JULIA  Twenty-one years I've given to him. Twenty-one years

MILLIE  Given to whom?

JULIA  Franklin. Who else?  (*Crosses to* MILLIE ) Millie, you're not suggesting I've given anyone else any of those twenty-one years?  I've been a rock of faithfulness, a regular Lot's wife, and now I'm turning to salt right in front of you.

MILLIE  You and Franklin have had a fight?

JULIA  If I ever speak to him again, it will be a fight they put on paid TV.

MILLIE  (*Crosses* R *of desk*) A lot seems to have happened in the two weeks I was in New York

JULIA  Too much has happened  I don't know how to tell you.

MILLIE. Why don't you try?

JULIA  I should have written an anonymous letter and signed it Furious  Then you would have answered it in your column and never known it was I

MILLIE  (*Sits* R *of desk*) Then tell me about it as if it were a letter

JULIA  That's a marvelous idea  (*Sits* L *of desk* ) Dear Millie . . . Oh, I feel so silly

MILLIE  Go on, Julia

JULIA. Dear Millie, I've never written to a column like this before but— (*Rises and goes* U C) I can't

MILLIE  Why not?

JULIA  You're too old a friend  I feel ridiculous.

MILLIE  Perhaps you'd better ask someone else's advice

JULIA  (*Eager to continue*) Oh, no, you're the professional

MILLIE  Then go ahead

JULIA  Well, I don't know when it all began but I only found out last week

MILLIE  Found out what, Julia?

JULIA  That—no, I can't. I can't tell you  (*Goes* U C )

MILLIE  (*Rises*) No, I don't think you can  Why don't you go home and write me about it?

JULIA. (*Comes back*) But I shall  (MILLIE *sits smiling* ) Prepare yourself, Millie. My husband, Franklin, is having an affair with Eloise

MILLIE  Julia, do you know what you're saying?

JULIA  I shall repeat it  My husband—

MILLIE  I heard you the first time

JULIA  Twenty-one years I've given to that man

MILLIE  Julia, we've already had the statistics

JULIA  (*Crosses above desk and leans on it*) Well, it's true and now he's sneaking out to see Eloise  My friend, our friend  Oh, Millie, I don't believe it

MILLIE  Neither do I  Why don't you just forget it?  It's probably not true

JULIA  But it is!  I know it is!  I saw them at Lookout Rock

MILLIE  *You* saw *them* at Lookout Rock?

JULIA  (*Sits* L *of desk*) They didn't see me, of course  That would have been too embarrassing

MILLIE  What were you doing there?

JULIA  My homework

MILLIE  Your homework?

JULIA  I'm taking art classes now

MILLIE  I didn't know.

JULIA  Yes I've always had a natural artistic bent

MILLIE  Who knows, you might be another Grandma Moses

JULIA  Not for a few years yet, I hope  Anyway, I was sketching this magnificent elm tree

MILLIE  From the parking lot at Lookout Rock?

JULAI  No  I couldn't get the proper angle on it from there  I went down the path quite a ways  I was just filling in my cobalt for the leaves—

MILLIE  Cobalt leaves?

JULIA  What's wrong with that?

MILLIE  Cobalt is blue, Julia

JULIA  Oh? (*For a moment she is at a loss for words*) Well, so are my leaves  I'm studying impressionistic painting  (*Rises*) I paint what I see, not what is there  Anyone can do that.

MILLIE  Then why did you have to go to Lookout Rock to paint a tree that isn't the way it looks?

JULIA  (*Crosses c*) Millie, you're splitting hairs  I have to look at it to see the way *I* see it so I can paint it the way it isn't  So, as I was saying, I was painting my green leaves and suddenly there was this beautiful chirping sound

MILLIE  It was Eloise with Franklin?

JULIA  No, it was a yellow-throated thing

MILLIE  Barn-swallow?

JULIA  I suppose so  So I took up my binoculars—

MILLIE  You carry binoculars in your paint kit?

JULIA  I'm recording secretary of the bird watchers of Lower Greenville County, aren't I?

MILLIE  Of course  Go on

JULIA  I slipped my binoculars up to my eye and there he was—

MILLIE  Franklin?

JULIA  The bird! (*Crosses below sofa*) I recorded it in my log book and I was bringing my glasses down from the branch and what did I see there under the tree?

MILLIE  I give up

JULIA  Franklin and Eloise  They were drinking martinis.

MILLIE  Under a tree in the middle of the woods?

JULIA  You know how sophisticated Franklin is  He always must have his creature comforts  And he had mixed them just the way I like them—no olive but an onion *(Sits on the sofa )*

MILLIE  *(Rises)* What did you do?

JULIA  I was in a state of shock  I spilled my cobalt all down my good Lord and Taylor smock and ran for the car  I don't know how I ever got back to the house  Tears were running down my checks

MILLIE  *(Moves to the sofa)* Did you speak to Franklin when he came in?

JULIA  He went right upstairs and took a nap  When he came down, I was cool  Glacial

MILLIE  He didn't admit anything?

JULIA. They never do

MILLIE  *(Sits next to JULIA on sofa)* Have you said anything to Eloise?

JULIA  I wanted to talk to you first, Millie  Should I confront her with it?

MILLIE  Or tell her husband?

JULIA  Tell Fred? Never! He's happy, let him stay that way  The irony of it is that Eloise has stolen her excuse to get out of the house from me

MILLIE  What excuse?

JULIA  She says she's taking art lessons  She couldn't even cover a wall with a paint roller  Remember when we all made posters for the Labor Day Dance last year? Hers was so bad, we had to post it in that dreadful diner behind the pinball machine where no one would possibly ever see it

MILLIE  Maybe she has hidden talent

JULIA  Well, it's certainly not for painting  *(Rises and crosses* D L *)* I should have become suspicious when Franklin said he was going to help old Mr Beebee

MILLIE  The one who broke his leg?

JULIA  That's the one  *(Moves above sofa )* Franklin said he'd go out and catch butterflies for Mr Neenee's collection  Oh, that was clever  Out where there was no phone to trap him  Well, he was running around with his net all right, but it wasn't butterflies he was after. It was that vulture Eloise  (*Crosses* U C ) What have I done to deserve this?

MILLIE  Nothing, Julia  You've done precisely *nothing* and that's why you deserve it

JULIA  (*Moves* D C ) What do you mean?

MILLIE  If Franklin has strayed from your nest, then you haven't kept it very well feathered

JULIA  Are you insinuating—?

MILLIE  (*Rises and crosses to* JULIA) Let's look at the facts, Julia  Franklin works in town all Summer, he comes up here week-ends and for his two weeks' vacation. How do you treat him when he's here?

JULIA  (*Crosses to desk*) Just like I do during the winter

MILLIE  Precisely. Do you start his day off with a good breakfast?

JULIA  You know perfectly well your Betty's sister, Petula, works for us  She's an excellent cook—

MILLIE  Well, adequate

JULIA  (*Sits* L *of desk*) Franklin eats very well.

MILLIE  But does he eat alone?

JULIA  He plays golf, Millie. You certainly don't expect me get up at seven-thirty in the morning and eat with him just so he can rush off and be at the Club by nine?

MILLIE  How about lunch?

JULIA  He never comes home for lunch

MILLIE  Why should he? Maybe he doesn't like carrot juice, tiger's milk, and cottage cheese staring up at him from a little round plate

JULIA  This is all beside the point  Eloise is stealing my husband from me and all you do is sit there and say what's the matter with *me*

MILLIE  You asked for my advice. (*Doorbell rings* )

JULIA  (*Rises*) Someone's here

MILLIE  (*Crosses above desk*) Would you rather I sent them away?

JULIA.  No. I must think. (*Crosses below desk to **French*** *windows* ) I'll just slip out in the garden. (BETTY *crosses from* R *to* L.)

MILLIE  It's getting a bit crowded  Why don't you go down to the left by the zinnias and marigolds?  I think that's still free and clear. (JULIA *exits* )

ELOISE  (*Off Stage* L )  Betty, did Mrs Tyson get home yet?

BETTY  (*Off Stage* L )  Yes, Ma'am  She's in the living room

ELOISE  (*Off Stage*)  I'll go right in

BETTY  (*Off Stage*)  I'd better hurry back to my kitchen floor  I'm trying that new one-step wax  I'm on the fourth step and the end isn't in sight  (BETTY *runs through from* L *to* R )

ELOISE  (*Comes in  She is calmer than the others have been*)  Millie, darling, I'm so glad you're back

MILLIE  (*Crosses to* ELOISE *and they kiss cheeks*)  I'm glad to be out of the heat

ELOISE  Did you have a successful trip?

MILLIE  Very  Signed the contracts for the paperback edition

ELOISE  Congratulations  You must be making a fortune now.

MILLIE  I'm doing all right

ELOISE  (*Crosses below the sofa and takes a cigarette from her purse*)  You ought to take a vacation, Millie  We ought to go off together  Just the two of us  (*Sits on sofa* )  That's why I've come to see you  (*Lights her cigarette* )

MILLIE  We haven't taken a vacation together since we went to Washington to see the cherry blossoms and they were rained out the day before

ELOISE  I mean, a longer vacation than a week-end. Millie, could you get six weeks off?

MILLIE  (*Moves above sofa*)  Six weeks?

ELOISE  You could write your column from out there and wire it in

MILLIE  (*Crosses* D L )  From where, Eloise?  Where do you want to go?

ELOISE  Reno.

MILLIE  Nevada?

ELOISE  The Reno where you get divorces

MILLIE (*Starts to laugh*) Oh, Eloise (*Sits chair* D L)

ELOISE You think it's so funny?

MILLIE But you and Fred? You've always been so happy

ELOISE That's what I thought I've done my best I've sublimated myself to Fred and his interests I've made myself a drone and now to find out he's taken my youth and is throwing it aside like a rotten kumquat

MILLIE He's found someone else younger?

ELOISF No, that's the worst of it He's found someone older

MILLIE Maybe it's a mother complex

ELOISF Not that much older—seven weeks and three days older And it's my best friend, next to you, of course, dear

MILLIE You must mean Lucille

ELOISF (*Jumps up*) You knew! Everyone must know (*Crosses* C) I'm the laughing stock of the super market I'll never go there again even if they do give stamps

MILLIF I didn't know, Eloise But I did know Lucille is seven weeks and three days older than you are

ELOISE (*Flicks ash in desk ashtray*) I should have guessed something was going on this summer When Fred's been on vacation before, he's never taken days off to go and call on clients But I was so trusting I should have become suspicious because who would buy elevators in the country?

MILLIE A good point

ELOISE (*Moves* C) Not that he just sells single elevators He arranges for whole skyscrapers, you know that. Oh, Millie, I'm so naive I wish I'd never found out

MILLIF It must be interesting the way you did (*She smiles to herself*)

ELOISE I was snorkling—

MILLIF You were whating?

ELOISE Snorkling (*Sits on the sofa*) You go under the water and you have this glass mask over your face and you see the most divine plants and fish And there's this periscope thing you breathe through

MILLIE You were doing this snorkling thing for your art lessons?

ELOISE  How did you know?

MILLIE  There seems to be quite a fad of painting around here.

ELOISE  That's what Lucille tells Ford she's doing Taking art lessons And, Millie, you know she can't even fill the right numbers on those paintings you get at the hardware store

MILLIE  So you were snorkling—

ELOISE  In the Monowee River You know where it gets very wide and calm almost like a little lake?

MILLIE  Right below Lookout Rock

ELOISE  Exactly Right below Well, I was snorkling away studying the colors for my art lesson and I rounded the bend I came up for a little breather and there sitting on a ledge were Fred and Lucille as calm as you please having a picnic He was just spreading caviar on melba toast

MILLIE  What did you say?

ELOISE  I couldn't speak I swallowed half the Monowee River (*Puts her cigarette out on the table by the sofa*) They didn't see me, they were too engrossed in each other I submerged as quick as a nuclear submarine and paddled back around the bend It's a wonder I didn't drown My life flashed before me

MILLIE  Did you enjoy the show?

ELOISE  (*Rises*) I do believe you're making fun of me

MILLIE  I mean it, Eloise (*Rises*) Did you see your life with Fred? Did you see why you sent him into the arms of an older woman?

ELOISE  (*Crosses* c) I didn't send him anywhere I've always been a most attentive wife

MILLIE  Have you?

ELOISE  I've kept a beautiful house for him and a lovely apartment in the city I've entertained all those dreary business clients of his for years

MILLIE  I know

ELOISE  The point is, what about Lucille? Didn't we all grow up together? Didn't we even share our potsies when we played hopscotch? And now to do this to me?

MILLIE  (*Crosses to* ELOISE *at* c) You don't think you did it to yourself?

ELOISE (*Moves away to French windows*) You should be getting mad at Lucille You're not reacting properly

MILLIE You're not thinking properly.

ELOISE How?

MILLIE (*Crosses to L of desk*) Maybe Lucille takes an interest in something besides Fred's house and apartment Maybe she's interested in his work

ELOISE In elevators?

MILLIE He's quite an important man, Eloise He's not just a salesman He's an executive of a very large corporation What do you know about his business?

ELOISE (*Crosses below desk to L C*) What is there to know about elevators? They go up and down.

MILLIE Maybe Lucille understands or at least takes an interest in the business end of the ups and downs, the problems he has, the hopes he has for the company

ELOISE If she does, she must be bored to death

MILLIE Not at all Business is fascinating if you bother to learn it

ELOISE I never even like to play Monopoly

Jo (*Comes in from French windows*) Millie! I didn't know you'd come back yet

MILLIE Just a few minutes ago, but I've been rather busy ever since

Jo Hello, Mrs Matthews Millie, all the mail is here on the desk (*Crosses below desk to U C.*) We've got a lot of work to do, but I have to go out for a few minutes. All right?

MILLIE Of course, if you have to.

Jo It's very important I'll just run up and change Excuse me (*Goes off R*)

ELOISE You give her a lot of time off

MILLIE But sometimes she works half the night through I don't know where I'd be without Jo

ELOISE (*Crosses below sofa*) So, Millie, you think it's all my fault? Is that all you have to say?

MILLIE No I've plenty more but you'll have to wait a minute

ELOISE What for?

MILLIE I might as well say it all at once. (*Goes to*

*French windows and calls* ) Girls! You can come in now. Come along! Everyone out of the pool!

ELOISE Who's out there?

MILLIE (*Moves above desk*) Just some friends of yours

ELOISE It isn't Lucille, is it? I can't face her. If I faced that face, I'd slap it

JULIA (*Comes in French windows*) Millie, I've been thinking— Oh, Eloise (*Moves below desk to* C ) I haven't seen you around lately I understand you've been busy with art lessons

ELOISE Yes, Julia, I'm progressing very well

JULIA So I've heard (MILLIE *is obviously glancing at her mail and* ELOISE *and* JULIA *exchange a helpless look and gesture to each other Neither knows what is going on now* LUCILLE *comes in through French windows* )

LUCILLE Julia! I thought I saw you come in ahead of me Were you hiding in the garden?

JULIA I wasn't hiding anywhere, I was walking.

LUCILLE (*Crosses to* JULIA *at* C ) You're very good at hiding though

JULIA What does that mean?

MILLIE (*Comes between* JULIA *and* LUCILLE) Girls! Girls! Girls! You can stop it now

LUCILLE Stop what?

MILLIE The little act

ELOISE What act?

MILLIE Come on, now I've known all of you for more years than we'd care to admit, and I know when you're lying

JULIA Lying about what?

MILLIE Art classes, Lookout Rock, husbands carrying on with other women.

LUCILLE (*Crosses below desk*) What are you talking about?

MILLIE When you came in first, Lucille, I thought you were auditioning for "The Merchant of Venice" again. If I hadn't gotten the chicken pox, you never would have played that part.

LUCILLE That's not true

MILLIE At first, I believed your story but then, as usual,

you overplayed it. Julia was a lot better but her colors were a little off on her palette. Then Eloise  Oh, poor Eloise, that was the worst of all

ELOISE  I beg your pardon?

MILLIE  Snorkling  (*Crosses* D L *to* ELOISE ) Eloise, you can't swim. You certainly couldn't have snorkled with water wings on  You couldn't have submerged

ELOISE  (*Sits in chair* D L ) I never thought of that.

MILLIE  Just what did you expect to prove with all this suppposed husband-trading anyway?

JULIA  (*Moves to below sofa*) It was Eloise's idea

ELOISE  You're the one who said Millie was getting too conceited

MILLIE  Me, conceited?

ELOISF  About your column

MILLIE  I didn't mean to be

LUCILLE  (*Crosses up by* L *of desk*) The three of us do nothing, absolutely nothing, and you rush around getting out books and columns and going to cocktail parties with important people  Maybe we're a little jealous

MILLIE  (*Crosses* C ) And maybe I'm jealous of you  Did you ever stop to think of that?

JULIA  (*Sits on sofa*) Why would you be jealous?

MILLIE  Because you all have husbands, good ones, too. and I lost mine years ago  Don't you think I'd trade all this writing business to come home and have a good man sitting here waiting for me? Why, I'd throw my typewriter off Lookout Rock so fast—

LUCILLE  (*Sits chair* L *of desk*) Millie, I didn't think you might be jealous of us

JULIA  And you saw right through our practical joke?

MILLIE  Uh-huh

JULIA  Then why did you have to be so mean to me? You said I wasn't a good wife to Franklin  You said I didn't even feed him properly

LUCILLE  Millie said that? I've been dying to for ages. The way you treat him is disgraceful

JULIA  I suppose I could have breakfast with him and give him a man's lunch

MILLIE  Why don't you try it?

LUCILLF  If you do, I'll go on a self-improvement course

She told me I was going to pot like Bette Davis in those
movies where she stops caring about herself  You're right,
Millie. I admit it

JULIA  What about you, Eloise?  Did Millie say anything
to you ?

ELOISE  I suppose I might learn a little about Fred's
business  After all, he is a success and I really don t understand anything about elevators other than which button to
push

LUCILLE  You sure don't  (*Rises and crosses* D *a few
steps* )  It was years before I understood all about Ford's
stocks and bonds, but now I read the Wall Street Journal
faithfully.

MILLIE  Then maybe we've all learned a lesson from
our practical joke

ELOISE  Maybe we have

JO  (*Enters* U C *from* R  *She is dressed very nicely and
looks very chic  She carries a purse and wears a small hat
She comes* D *to* MILLIE *at* C )  Excuse me, but I'll be back
by five-thirty, Millie

MILLIE  Where are you off to ?

JO  (*As she opens purse and gets her gloves out*)  Something new I've started  I'm taking art lessons  Bye, now
(*She goes out* U C *and* L  *As she does, she puts her gloves
on and a piece of paper falls to the floor* C  *She leaves behind her a galvanized silence* )

ELOISE  Art lessons? Is she serious?

JULIA  (*Rises*)  She dropped some money  (*Picks up
paper* )  No, it's just a note  (*Glances at it* )  No ! I don't
believe it !

LUCILLE  (*Crosses* L *and grabs the note*)  What does it
say ?  (*Reads it* )  No !

ELOISE  (*Springs up and grabs the note*)  No !

MILLIE  (*Crosses above them to* D L *by* ELOISE)  Let me
have it !  (*Reads it aloud* )  "Darling  Meet me at Lookout
Rock as usual. I've gotten away from the wife "  It's signed
with the initial "F."

ELOISE  (*They look at each other for a moment*)  Fred !

JULIA  Franklin !

LUCILLE. Ford !

ELOISE (*Rushes* U C ) Quickly, girls. Let's go  Take my car.

LUCILLE  Hurry! (LUCILLE *and* JULIA *cross* U C )

MILLIE. Where are you going?

ELOISE  Lookout Rock  Whosever husband it is, we'll stop him before it's too late

JULIA  I've learned my lesson, Franklin

ELOISE  It's my fault. It's all my fault  Oh, Fred. I'll try to be a better wife.

LUCILLE  Ford, don't! Let's start over!

(*They have all been exiting and the lines carry them Off Stage and* L  MILLIE *sinks in chair* D L *in exhaustion as* JO *appears at the French windows* )

JO  How's that for action?

MILLIE (*Rises*) Jo, where did you come from?

JO (*Moves in* C ) I circled the house  Let them worry for a while and see if they like a practical joke

MILLIE (*Crosses to her at* C ) How did you know what was going on?

JO  I came in when Mrs  Matthews and Mrs  Jamison were here before you got back  They looked funny when I came in so I took the woman's prerogative and eavesdropped  I was going to tell you but then I thought this would be more fun

MILLIE (*Laughs and moves to the French windows*) Jo, you're a genius. We'd better call them up tonight and have them all over for lunch and cocktails tomorrow to smooth it over.

JO  If you're going to do that, then you'll have to work through the night (*Picks up letters on the desk* )

MILLIE  I don't mind  This has been a day to remember

JO (*Sits* L *of desk*) And the first letter is signed "Troubled." (MILLIE *sits* R *of desk*  JO *reads* ) "Dear Millie  I have a problem  I think my wife is cheating on me. She says she is taking art lessons     ."

MILLIE. Oh, no! (*They both laugh as the curtain falls* )

# OTHER TITLES AVAILABLE FROM BAKER'S PLAYS

## KEEPSAKES

## Pat Cook

*Drama / 4m, 6f / Interior*

Ever look at a family portrait and wonder what those people, posed and smiling, are really like? This family portrait shows you the inner workings of the Rogers family – how they deal with everyday things, how they deal with both happy and sad events which effect each and every one of them. These funny, poignant and all-too-human characters go through life the best way they know how.

Austin does his best to keep the house running smoothly, unless he has to take Pawpaw's trunk out of the basement. Mary Jo is outwardly pleased when son Mitchell gets engaged to Tish but explains "They're too young!" Her sister, Brenda, helps out by saying "Not any younger than you were when you got married." Brenda's husband, Dale, has his own advice for young Mitchell – "Marriage consists in large part of just giving up!" And Pawpaw keeps hearing voices and seeing people who aren't there.

The very fabric of the family unit meets its ultimate challenge when Brenda and Dale have to move in with them. Daughter Jan has to put up with a whiney dog, Mitchell and Tish can't seem to find time to talk about their upcoming marriage and everyone is bunking up with everyone else, leaving the men to sleep on the couch – any of this sound familiar? Brought to you by the same author of *Good Help is So Hard to Murder.*